RETURN

Aaron Becker

WALKER BOOKS
AND SUBSIDIARIES
LONDON · BOSTON · SYDNEY · AUCKLAND

For my parents

Special thanks to Natalie Moss for her assistance
with the petroglyph design in this book, and to
mis compañeros de erranT in Granada, Spain, for
opening their doors to an artist from far away.

First published 2016 by Walker Books Ltd
87 Vauxhall Walk, London SE11 5HJ

This edition published 2017

10 9 8 7 6 5 4 3 2 1

© 2016 Aaron Becker

The right of Aaron Becker to be identified as
author/illustrator of this work has been
asserted by him in accordance with the
Copyright, Designs and Patents Act 1988

Printed in China

British Library Cataloguing in Publication Data:
a catalogue record for this book is available from
the British Library

ISBN 978-1-4063-7329-5

www.walker.co.uk

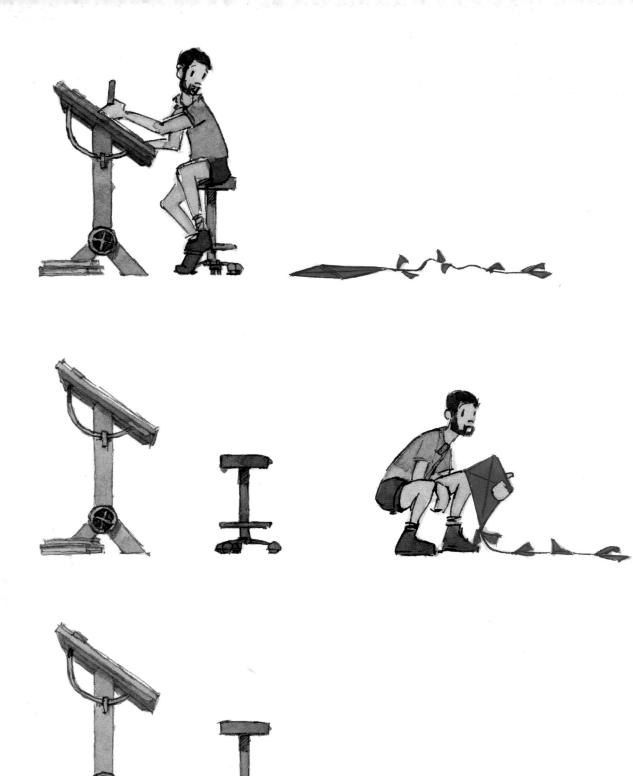